This paperback edition first published in 2012 by Andersen Press Ltd.
First published in Great Britain in 1986 by Andersen Press Ltd.,
20 Vauxhall Bridge Road, London SW1V 2SA.
Published in Australia by Random House Australia Pty.,
Level 3, 100 Pacific Highway, North Sydney, NSW 2060.
Copyright © Tony Ross, 1986.
The rights of Tony Ross to be identified
as the author and illustrator of this work have been asserted by him
in accordance with the Copyright, Designs and Patents Act, 1988.
All rights reserved.
Colour separated in Switzerland by Photolitho AG, Zürich.
Printed and bound in Malaysia by Tien Wah Press.

10   9   8   7   6   5   4   3

British Library Cataloguing in Publication Data available.
ISBN 978 1 84939 446 8

This book has been printed on acid-free paper.

A Little Princess Story

I Want My Potty!

Tony Ross

Andersen Press

"Nappies are YUUECH!" said the Little Princess.
"There MUST be something better!"

"The potty's the place," said the Queen.

At first the Little Princess thought the potty
was worse.

"THE POTTY'S THE PLACE!" said the Queen.

So . . . the Little Princess had to learn.

Sometimes the Little Princess was a long way from the potty when she needed it most.

Sometimes the Little Princess played tricks on the potty . . .

. . . and sometimes the potty played tricks on the
Little Princess.

Soon the potty was fun

and the Little Princess loved it.

Everybody said the Little Princess was clever and
would grow up to be a wonderful queen.

"The potty's the place!" said the
Little Princess proudly.

One day the Little Princess was playing at the top
of the castle . . . when . . .

"I WANT MY POTTY!" she cried.

"She wants her potty," cried the Maid.

"She wants her potty," cried the King.

"She wants her potty," cried the Cook.

"She wants her potty," cried the Gardener.

"She wants her potty," cried the General.

"I know where it is," cried the Admiral.

So the potty was taken as quickly as possible

to the Little Princess . . .

. . . just a little too late.

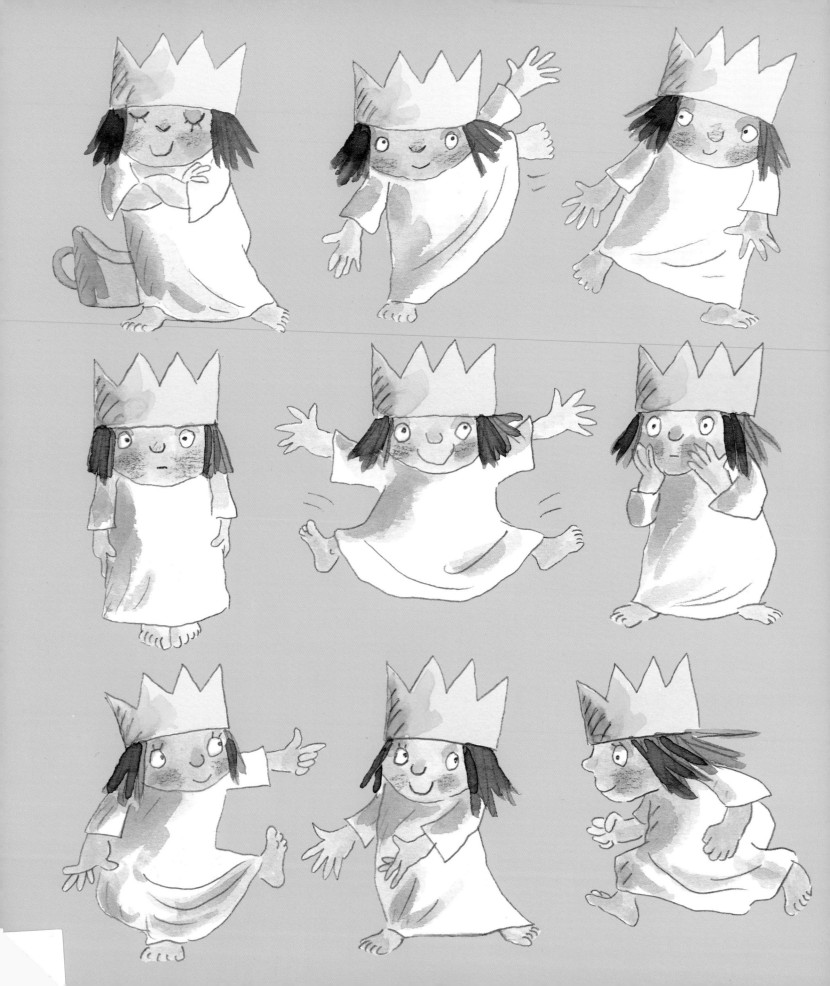

Other Little Princess Books

I Want My Dinner!

I Want My Dummy!

I Want My Light On!

I Want My Present!

I Want a Friend!

I Want to Go Home!

I Want Two Birthdays!

I Want to Do It by Myself!

I Want to Win!

I Want My Dummy!

I Don't Want to Go to Hospital!

I Don't Want to Wash My Hands!

LITTLE PRINCESS TV TIE-INS

Can I Keep It?

I Want My New Shoes!

I Don't Want a Cold!

I Want My Tent!

Fun in the Sun!

I Want to Do Magic!

I Want a Trumpet!

I Want My Sledge!

I Don't Like Salad!

I Don't Want to Comb My Hair!

I Want a Shop!

I Want to Go to the Fair!

I Want to Be a Cavegirl!

I Want to Be a Pirate!

I Want to Be Tall!

I Want My Puppets!

I Want My Sledge! Book and DVD